For Poppy

www.mascotbooks.com

Love Your Pony, Love Your Planet

For more information, please contact:
Mascot Books
560 Herndon Parkway #120
Herndon, VA 20170
info@mascotbooks.com

CPSIA Code: PRT0813A
ISBN-10: 1620863030
ISBN-13: 9781620863039

Printed in the United States

I♥VE YOUR PONY
I♥VE YOUR PLANET

All About Pony Poo
and Other Helpful Things We Can Do!

Hi! My name is Happy.
Follow me through the book to learn how to take the best care of your pony and our planet. Look for the key words and use the glossary to help you too!

It is important to take the **BEST** care of your pony. Some things we do can hurt our pony. There are many ways you can love your pony without hurting the beautiful planet we call home.

So let's learn how we can protect our natural resources such as water, soil and plants.

Wait! Read more before you spray!

Have you ever heard of the word *eco-friendly*?

The word eco means "earth" and the word friendly means "to be nice". So *eco-friendly* means "to be nice to the earth".

Do you know what a blue ribbon is?
A blue ribbon means the BEST in show!
Look for this symbol on the pages of this book.

If you see it on a page, it means
this is the BEST way to take care of your pony
in an *eco-friendly* way!

Let's talk about *Best Management Practices*
or *BMPs* for short!

BMPs are *eco-friendly* things people can do
or use that don't hurt the planet.

BMPs for your pony include things for his diet,
his grooming and his home.

BMPs for the farm include things for the pasture,
the water and the barn.

By feeding, grooming and housing
your pony correctly, you show him your love.

The first *BMP* we will look at is your pony's diet.

Too much food and your pony will get too chubby…

Not enough food and your pony will get too skinny…

A pony is best at eating
a *fiber-based* diet like grass and hay.
This *natural* diet also has the least
negative *impact* (or hurt) on the Earth.

So the first thing you can do to take the
BEST care of your pony and the BEST care
of the planet is to feed him a *natural* diet
of good grass or good hay.

Do you know how you feel when you eat too much candy?

We need to be careful with ponies because they can eat too much grass and get sick.

Grass has sugar in it just like candy, so if ponies eat too much they can get sick.

This sickness is called *founder* and it is really sad to see a pony with it.

This pony needs a diet and his feet show a history of *founder*.

Have you ever seen a pony in a muzzle?

A muzzle is the BEST tool you can use if your pony gets too chubby from eating grass, because the muzzle allows him to eat, but not too much.

The BEST thing to do if your pony gets fat on hay is to use a *slow feeder*.

A slow feeder is a way to feed your pony so he doesn't eat too much.

Slow feeders make ponies less bored, more happy and less likely to eat too much.

REMEMBER!
A FIBER DIET SHOULD BE BALANCED WITH VITAMINS AND MINERALS!

Do you take a vitamin each day?

It is important that you take vitamins
to grow and feel your BEST!

Your pony is the same!
Ponies need vitamins to feel their BEST!

What about the planet? Aren't we learning how to take the BEST care of our pony AND the planet?

How is a *fiber* diet BEST for the planet?

When you have *energy,*
you want to run and play. The planet
has *energy* called *fossil fuels* that we use
for a bunch of things. Natural gas, coal
and oil are *fossil fuels.* Just like you can
run out of *energy,* the earth can too.

A *fiber* based diet for your pony helps the planet save *energy*! Want to know how? It is like a math problem.

Did you say MATH?

Yup! First you need to know that feed takes *energy* to be made. So that is the beginning of our math problem…

The problem starts with the *energy* it takes to grow grains for feed.

 PLUS the *energy* used to harvest grains

 PLUS the *energy* it takes to get the grain to the mill.

WAIT…
we're not done!

 PLUS the *energy* it takes for the mill to turn the grain into feed.

 PLUS the *energy* it takes for the mill to get the feed to the store.

 PLUS the *energy* it takes for you to get the feed from the store to your barn!

 Total amount of *energy* for feed!

That equals a lot of *energy!*

The earth's *energy* is being used up too fast, so it is BEST to follow a diet that requires the least amount of *energy*, like hay and pasture.

Can you see why that would be a problem? Oh wait! You can't see anything with that hair!

Energy use is only one part of the problem.

Crops like grains need more *chemicals* to make them grow than hay or pasture need. Chemicals are not *eco-friendly*.

Guess where the *chemicals* go that aren't used by the crops!

Chemicals can wash off the land and into the water.

This can kill the fish and plants in the water and can make water unsafe to drink or play in.

But it's not just *chemicals* for crops that we need to be concerned about.

Products made for grooming your pony can also contain *chemicals* that harm the planet.

That shampoo can wash right down the drain!

There are products to use when grooming and bathing your pony that show love for the planet. They are called *organic* and *biodegradable*.

This means that they are made from plants and minerals instead *chemicals*.

What makes them the BEST products?

Because plant and mineral products don't hurt the water, dirt and all the critters that live there.

We've learned how we can love our ponies and the planet by how we feed and groom them.

Now let's see how we can show our love for our ponies and planet when we take care of their health and their home.

We will start with health...

There are two kinds of pests that can hurt your pony. *External pests* bother the outside of your pony like flies, mosquitoes and rodents (mice and rats). *Internal pests* hurt the inside of your pony. Worms are *internal pests*.

Eco-friendly ways are the BEST ways to deal with both.

Don't worry, I can see!

BEST

The BEST *natural* ways to keep *external pests* off your pony are *organic* fly spray, fly masks and fly sheets.

Natural pest catchers like fly-predator wasps, bats and birds can help with biting pests because they eat them for food. One way to attract birds and bats is to put up bird houses and bat houses near your barn.

Flies are not as active at night so turning your pony out at night helps keep flies away too.

Dumping any water from extra buckets and tubs is one of the BEST ways to help keep mosquitos away.

It is BEST to keep the barn extra clean and pick up dropped feed. This will help keep mice and rats away as they carry and spread disease.

A barn cat is also a *natural* way to reduce rodent pests.

Now we have learned the BEST ways to treat *external* (outside) *pests*.

Do you know who is the BEST
at treating *internal pests*?
It happens to be your VETS!

Hey,
that rhymes!

But there are some *natural*
and *eco-friendly* things you
can do to help!

First, ask your vet to do a test for internal worms so you are not using more medicine (*chemicals*) than you really need to.

Also, it's BEST to ask your vet to put the used worming syringe into a sealed plastic bag before they throw it away.

That way any leftover medicine won't get into water through the dirt.

Now that we have learned about diet, grooming and health, let's look at your pony's home.

Where can we show our love around the farm?

GOOD QUESTION!

On the farm we can look at the pasture, the manure pile and the water sources. Let's start with the pasture!

Taking the BEST care of your pasture
is very important because it can
provide a healthy diet for your pony.

Your pony's pasture will need to rest after it
is used for your pony's food. Moving your
pony from a grazed-down pasture to a rested
pasture is called *rotational grazing*.

Keeping out weeds is also important. The BEST way to fight weeds is to give the grass what it needs to be a thick and healthy pasture.

Weeds are also not good for your pony. If you keep your pasture grass healthy, you won't need to use *chemicals* to fight weeds.

Another thing that can hurt the planet is your pony's manure. So here is the scoop on pony poop! A pony can make 15-20 pounds of poop EVERY DAY!

Manure can have worm eggs,
weed seeds, *chemicals* from weed
killer and *bacteria* (germs) in it.

Manure contains other things that can really hurt the planet. All the things in your pony's food that get used by the body are called *nutrients*. The *nutrients* that aren't used end up in the manure. If too many *nutrients* get into the water, they can kill the fish.

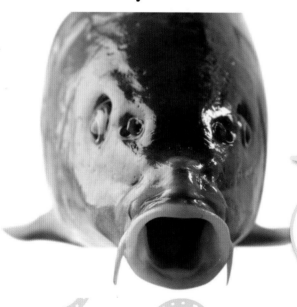

Help! I can't breathe!

What are the BEST things to do to make sure the bad things in manure don't reach the dirt and the water?

You can start by cleaning up your pony's poo, and putting it in a storage bin or a covered manure *stack pile*.

The BEST manure storage bin has sides and a solid floor. Solid sides and floors will keep the manure in place. The BEST place for manure storage is far away from any water.

The BEST bins or piles are covered
with a roof or tarp to keep storm
water from falling into it.

This way, the storm water won't
cause the bad things in manure to
run-off into the soil and water.

Have you ever heard of *composting*?
It is the BEST way to get the bad stuff out
of the manure. Little things called *microbes*
live in manure. They are made up of good
bacteria, earthworms and other things
that help get rid of the bad stuff.

WORMS
ARE
COOL!

The *microbes* and worms reduce the amount of manure and the amount of bad things in it! Composting is not easy, but it is worth it!

Before

After

Rain can also flow through paddocks and through manure piles. It can create mud in the paddocks and pick up dirt and manure and take it to nearby water.

Look at all this mud!

Speaking of water...do you have a stream or pond on your farm?

It's important to keep your pony out of any streams or ponds too.

A fence is the BEST way to do this.

Nobody would want their pony to drink from water that had manure in it!

Remember!

You will need to make sure your pony has another source of clean water. Water tanks filled with fresh, clean water are a great way to make sure your pony drinks enough water!

They really LOVE me!

Another way to keep nearby water clean is by using a gutter system on the barn.

This will carry the water away from the paddocks with manure and stop it from picking up germs.

But where else can the water go?

It can go into a *rain garden*!

A *rain garden BMP* is an area with special soil and plants to soak up rain water.

You can also use a *rain barrel* on the gutter to collect the water. This water can be *recycled* and used for watering plants or bathing your pony.

That also saves water!

I bet if you take a look around your barn you will find other ways to show your planet some love!

Can you think of any?

Remember *energy*?

When you save *energy* around your farm, you show your planet love! So how about turning your lights and fans on a timer? How about using solar (sun) power for fencing? How about *recycling*?

How does recycling save *energy*?

It takes *energy* to make new things. By re-using things we save *energy*.

How many things do you *recycle*? Can you think of more ways to *recycle*? Here are some ideas for *recycling* around the barn and farm…

What about using old tubs for feed buckets?

What about
tires?

What about
hay strings?

What about
horse shoes?

Don't forget your riding equipment and clothes! If someone uses your old stuff, there will be less *energy* needed for making new stuff!

This bridle is covered in mold! They must not use it.

Remember, there are a lot of ways to LOVE both your PONY and your PLANET!

Let's review what we learned…

We show our PONY love with the BEST diet, grooming, health care and housing!

We show our PLANET love by using less *energy*, more *organic* products and by protecting the water and *natural resources*!

Show your LOVE by leaving kisses on your pony and only hoofprints on the planet!

Glossary

Bacteria - very small living things that you cannot see. Some kinds of bacteria cause diseases (sickness) but most are helpful and used for good things.

Balanced Diet - all the things your pony needs to eat to be healthy (not sick).

Best Management Practice - things people can do or use to reduce pollution (hurt to the planet).

Biodegradable - something that is able to go back into the planet. Paper is biodegradable, but plastic is not.

Chemicals - in this book the chemicals we are talking about are pesticides (stuff that kills pests, like bugs) and herbicides (stuff that kills plants).

Composting - the activity of mixing natural things in a bin so it rots and becomes gooey.

Eco-Friendly - eco means "earth" and friendly means "nice". So eco-friendly is something that is nice to the earth.

Energy - the power to run things like electricity for lights, gas for cars and coal to heat houses.

External Pests - things that bug your pony on the outside like flies and mice.

Fiber - a small, thin part of a plant that is shaped like a thread. It is an important part of a pony's diet.

Founder - a problem with a pony's hoof. To founder is to sink. In a pony with founder, the bone in the hoof sinks.

Impact - something that can affect the planet. Pony manure can negatively impact (hurt a lot) water if it gets in it.

Internal Pests - these are things that bug your pony from inside of him. Parasites (worms) are internal pests.

Microbes - little tiny things (like bugs) that get into the manure during composting that help it rot.

Natural Resource - things that are from nature are called natural. Things that we use are resources. So natural resources are things we use from nature.

Nutrient - something in food that helps people, animals and plants live and grow.

Organic - a natural thing that is not treated with any chemicals.

Rain Barrel - really big, round drum that holds water. They can catch water off the roof so you can reuse the water.

Rain Garden - a place that rain water can go to soak into the ground. Extra thirsty, special plants and soil are used in a rain garden.

Recycle - to use something again, sometimes in a different way. Reusing pony shoes and making hooks is recycling.

Rotational Grazing - this is when we move our pony from one pasture to another. The pastures are taking turns.

Slow Feeder - a way to feed your pony so he eats slow so he doesn't get too full and get a belly ache.

Stack Pile - a place where all the pony poo is put after you clean his stall. Each day the poo is put on top of the pile (stacked) until it gets big.

ABOUT THE AUTHOR

Laura Batts, MS, PAS comes from a long line of horse lovers; her great-grandfather owned a livery stable and her grandmother was an avid equestrian. Her love for the planet was a result of a deep appreciation of nature instilled in her by her mother.

Laura raised her four children on a horse farm where she gained extensive equine experience as a professional trainer, instructor and judge. She continues to ride and shares her love for horses with her grandchildren.

For years, Laura held a position at a leading equestrian retailer and as a professional equine nutritionist. In both positions, she helped horse owners learn how take the best care of their horses. She visited hundreds of farms and witnessed over and over the mud, manure and chemicals that can exist on a horse farm.

Laura recognized a need and recently she obtained a graduate degree in environmental science and started her equine educational business. She has written this book with the youngest equestrian in mind. Currently she is working on two additional books, a smart phone app and an extensive educational program...all in the hope of helping the three "Ps": people, ponies and the planet.

www.HappyHorseHealthyPlanet.com

Acknowledgements

I would like to thank the following people for their help with this book.

My father, for instilling in me a belief that I can accomplish anything. My children and grandchildren, the reasons for everything I do. My soul sistas Sally, Karen, Sue and Amy, for their honesty and unending support. My wonderful siblings, for their encouragement. All my horsey friends (two and four legged), for teaching me so much about the love affair between people and horses.

And of course, to my husband Martin, the rock on which my life is built, for believing in my dream and helping me follow my bliss.

I would be remiss in not acknowledging Brad and William for never giving up until we got it right, and Laura V. for her patience with a first-time author.

I would also like to acknowledge the following people and companies for providing many of the wonderful photos used in the book:

Greta Corkran
Amy Trout
Karen Holthaus
The Bakers
Stockbridge School of Agriculture
Westgate Labs
Espree Horse Products
Parmak USA
O_2 Compost Systems